CURLY DOG'S
JUMP AROUND
MUSIC COUNTDOWN

JENNY AND RANDALL SCOTT MURPHY

www.1000storybooks.com

DEDICATION

For our family and our beloved rescue dog, Curly. Please consider getting a rescue dog for your family.

Hello!

Curly Dog is happy to see you!

She loves wearing costumes and dancing (it's more like jumping around) to her favorite songs.

Will you help her learn to count down from 10?
She gets stuck and needs help now and then.

You will. That's exciting!

Turn the page to see Curly's first costume and song...

DJ Curly is in the house!

She spins around and drops a bouncy sound.

Curly makes it number 10 on her countdown.

It's Leighanne Llama with the song "Pajama Momma."

Curly is counting backwards from 10.
Help her start the countdown by saying 10.

10!

Turn the page to see Curly's next costume and song...

It's Zookeeper Curly!

What's the next number counting down from 10?
Curly says 8.
Wait a second, Curly. Think again.

Do you know what number should be next?

9?

Correct! Thanks for your help.

Curly has her next song.
A toe-tapper from The Talking Bears can't be wrong.

Count with Curly Dog.

10, 9...

Turn the page for Curly's costume change.

Karate Curly says hi-yah!

10, 9...
Now, Curly says 8.
Good job, Curly!

Number 8 has a good beat,
It's Bruno Cars with "Stinky Feet Don't Smell Sweet."

10, 9, 8...
What's next?

7?
You are really doing well!

What will we see now?

It's T-Rex Curly! Can you roar like a T-Rex?

Very good!

Curly's number 7 song is "Dinosaurs Dance In The City."

Curly dedicates it to her friend Griffy.

10, 9, 8, 7...

We are on a roll, friend!

Superhero Curly just landed!

10, 9, 8, 7...
What's next?

6?

You are a counting superhero!

The next tasty tune is by Toast Malone,
It's called "Superheroes Give Dogs Treats and Bones."

Do you think Curly Dog likes treats and bones?

Of course!

It's Grandma Curly!

10, 9, 8, 7, 6...
Help Curly remember what's next.

5? Hurray! You did it!

Curly plays a song by Silly Eyelash.

It's called "I Saw Grandma's Underpants When She Tried To Dance."

What Curly will we see next?

Hey, dude. It's Surfer Curly!

10, 9, 8, 7, 6, 5...

Curly Dog says the next number is 3.
Oh my, Curly needs a little help from you and me.

Do you know what's next?

4? Correct!

Surfer Curly's song is by Jay-T

She hip hops, be-bops and then...
Belly flops! Silly Curly Dog!

How now, it's Curly the Cow!

10, 9, 8, 7, 6, 5, 4...

What's next?

Three?

Cowabunga!

Can you moo like a cow?

Excellent!

Curly plays a song by Carrie Understood.
It makes Curl Girl twirl and feel so good!

Rock Star Curly takes the stage!

10, 9, 8, 7, 6, 5, 4, 3...

What's next?

2?

Correct. You're a counting rock star!

Curly blows her fans a kiss...

And plays the song "Eating Fruit Makes Me Toot" by Happy Hair Angi and Uncle Chris!

It's Princess Curly!

10, 9, 8, 7, 6, 5, 4, 3, 2...

Can you believe it, friend?
We've almost counted all the way backwards from 10!

Curly is at number 1 on her jump around (and sometimes belly flop) music countdown!

What will happen next?

You are a fast page turner!

Magician Curly is here to play a hit.

Number one is "Drinking My Juicebox In Fuzzy Sox" by Taylor Gift.

Music has magic, that's true.
Especially when it's shared with friends like you.

Count with Curly one more time...

She wants to give you a special surprise.

10

9

8

7

6

5

4

3

2

1...

TURN THE PAGE FOR A SPECIAL SURPRISE

Surprise!

It's a special Curly hug. Curly Dog loves you!

ABOUT THE AUTHOR

Jenny and Randall Scott Murphy love kids, reading, music, and their rescue dog, Curly. Curly protects the husband and wife team from pesky squirrels and rowdy vacuum cleaners in and around their Austin home. Curly helped raise their two grown sons, Jordan and Griffin. Jenny works for the University of Texas at Austin. Scott writes the bestselling Fun Stories series of short story humor books for grownups under the pen name R. Scott Murphy.

Made in the USA
Monee, IL
06 February 2022

90746704R00021